Dear Parents,

Welcome to the Scholastic Reader series. We have taken over 80 years of experience with teachers, parents, and children and put it into a program that is designed to match your child's interests and skills.

Level 1—Short sentences and stories made up of words kids can sound out using their phonics skills and words that are important to remember.

Level 2—Longer sentences and stories with words kids need to know and new "big" words that they will want to know.

Level 3—From sentences to paragraphs to longer stories, these books have large "chunks" of texts and are made up of a rich vocabulary.

Level 4—First chapter books with more words and fewer pictures.

It is important that children learn to read well enough to succeed in school and beyond. Here are ideas for reading this book with your child:

- Look at the book together. Encourage your child to read the title and make a prediction about the story.
- Read the book together. Encourage your child to sound out words when appropriate. When your child struggles, you can help by providing the word.
- Encourage your child to retell the story. This is a great way to check for comprehension.
- Have your child take the fluency test on the last page to check progress.

Scholastic Readers are designed to support your child's efforts to learn how to read at every age and every stage. Enjoy helping your child learn to read and love to read.

—Francie Alexander
Chief Education Officer
Scholastic Education

To Rachel and Joey
— G.M.

Text copyright © 1994 by Grace Maccarone.
Illustrations copyright © 1994 by Meredith Johnson.
Activities copyright © 2003 Scholastic Inc.

All rights reserved. Published by Scholastic Inc.
SCHOLASTIC, CARTWHEEL BOOKS, and associated logos are trademarks
and/or registered trademarks of Scholastic Inc.

Library of Congress Cataloging-in-Publication Data is available.

ISBN 0-590-48369-2

30 29 28 27   15/0
Printed in the U.S.A.   40
First printing, August 1994

SOCCER GAME!

by Grace Maccarone
Illustrated by Meredith Johnson

Scholastic Reader — Level 1

SCHOLASTIC INC.

New York Toronto London Auckland Sydney
Mexico City New Delhi Hong Kong Buenos Aires

We start the game.

We're ready.

We aim.

We pass.

We fall.

They get the ball.

Away they go!

We're doomed!
Oh, no!

It's in the air.

Our goalie is there!

We dribble.

We pass.

We slip
on the grass.

We kick. We run.

We're having fun!

We see a hole.

We run to the goal.

The ball goes in.

Hooray! We win!